PRAIS

THE DISAPPEARANCE OF TOM NERO

TJ Price's deceptively loose meta approach is a dark joy. It lets the horror creep in, as though from the fibers of the paper in Tom's journal. *The Disappearance of Tom Nero* is crumbling mental disintegration effectively rendered and haunted by a unique demon. Recommended...and perhaps literally infectious.
Michael Wehunt, author of Greener Pastures

TJ Price's *The Disappearance of Tom Nero* is a mysterious labyrinth of a story exploring themes of identity and obsession. I loved the blend of metafiction and folklore and came away feeling quite unnerved. Much recommended!
Christi Nogle, author of The Best of Our Past, The Worst of Our Future

The Disappearance of Tom Nero is a linguistic parasite that slips into every decision you have ever made or will ever make. The skin of Tom's haunted doodles will replace your own, some days. And there are words that loom in this piece that elicit a sneaking suspicion only the sleepless have of their ominously still chairs. *The Disappearance of Tom Nero* is an infohazard that no one should read if they value their screb.
RSL

The Disappearance of Tom Nero uses metafiction as effortlessly as punctuation. Price's ambitious novelette is high concept weird fiction that operates simultaneously as literary experiment and character study. To say it sticks with you—much like its central conceit—is an understatement.
Carson Winter, author of Soft Targets

Deftly weaving dread through each transformation of the text, *The Disappearance of Tom Nero* lingers on the periphery of your consciousness long after you've set it down. Price's prose drips with a subtle paranoia that eventually drowns out every other sound."
Andrew F. Sullivan, author of The Marigold and The Handyman Method

The Disappearance of Tom Nero

TJ Price

SPOOKY
HOUSE
PRESS

The Disappearance of Tom Nero. Copyright © 2022 by TJ Price

First Edition

Cover design and cover copyright © 2023 by Leah Gharbaharan.

Interior design and formatting by Alexis Macaluso

Published by Spooky House Press, LLC.
East Islip, NY, 11730, USA
www.spookyhousepress.com

ISBN:
978-1-959946-10-6 (Paperback)
978-1-959946-11-3 (eBook)
Printed in the United States of America

to my beloved partner Matthew,
who keeps me from going missing

COMPOSITION BOOK

NON SUM QUALIS ERAM

100 Sheets • 200 Pages
9³/₄ in x 7¹/₂in (24.7cm x 19cm)
Wide Ruled

Friday, 8 October

I ink these thoughts down upon the page because
it strikes me that they may be of use to someone,
someday, who might be looking for me. I do think
that my fame will preclude me, and I imagine
these pages will be worth a pretty penny someday.
It chills me to even think that now, I am
involved in the creation of an heirloom perhaps
cherished object. I will take extra care not to
pill my drink upon the pages of this journal,
o keep it as pristine as possible (barring my
houghts, of course) for future generations.

   So much for that.
  This city never stops shouting at me. It's
like a needy toddler constantly underfoot,
reminding you of its presence. Everywhere you
look, somebody wants something, somebody needs
something, and most everybody has the difference
between the two confused. They say the city never
sleeps, but they didn't say it also suffered from
insomnia. It's like a noisy neighbor that keeps
you up until all hours, because theyre blasting
their infomercials through the thin wall. Not
that this has happened to me. Not recently,
anyway. I haven't had a home for a while now
I've been couch-surfing through the city. I know
just enough people from around here (though I've
had to draw on some pretty distant connections)
that I've been skating by. But the money, as they
say, is about to dry up, and I'm pretty sure
Ariel is done with me hanging around, especially

now that they've got the new beau. (Beaux?)
There's always the bar. I can get just drunk
enough to get interested in somebody, and
then, if I'm lucky, theyll want to go hang
out at "their place" (marijuana, hint hint)
and, well, that's one way I can procure a
roof for the evening. I'm not that ashamed of
it. I've met some interesting guys that way,
especially the morning after, and especially
if they don't remember who I am.

I've disappeared like that from many folks'
lives, over the years. In fact, I often
wonder: if I were to *actually* disappear, would
anyone be surprised? Would anyone even bother
to go looking?

I'm writing this as I spend my last clutch
of dollar bills on a PBR and a shot of
Doctor MacGillicuddy's Peppermint Schnapps.
Revolting, but at least it doesn't leave a
trail of itself down your throat after you're
done tasting it.

Most of the people who take lunch break
around here have a shot of it to mask the
beers or the Long Island Iced Teas.

Quickest I ever saw someone down a Long
Island Iced Tea: 13 seconds. That girl was in
and out, exact change, great tip, straighten
the hem of her work skirt, and back to

Cubicle Land she went. She stopped coming in one day. Vanished. Heard a rumor that she got fired. I wasn't there when she went. I often wonder if she had one last drink for the road.

So, like I said, people disappear. You gotta know that from the start, going in. At some point, everyone you surround yourself with goes away. Even if they don't want to.

Anyway, because I used to be a bartender, I think it proves that someone out there thought I had some kind of charisma. I know, and the world knows, that I'm an insufferable asshole, but I'm pretty smart about some things, and one of those things is booze, and another of those things is people.

Saturday, 9 October
As I was writing the prior entry, two things happened:

1)   The bartender, a petite but big-breasted woman wearing a t-shirt with the name of the bar (Kenny's Oasis) was accosted both physically and vocally by a large man wearing an apron. This, apparently, was Kenny, and she, Luz Gabriela was the bartender being fired, *despedida*, effective immediately.

2)   After Luz Gabriela stomped out of the bar, vowing some sort of revenge in Spanish, and

overhearing Kenny's predicament, I volunteered to
help him out for a shift behind the bar. I told
him I'd work for tips. He liked that part, and
a quick agreement was hashed out. As a result,
I netted about $150, which wasn't bad for a few
hours work, slinging drinks to the locals.

Obviously, this wasn't enough to get me into a
swanky hotel, but it was enough to get me a few
more drinks, and to make my way downtown to the
gay bars. In my favorite of them, I ran into an
old acquaintance, Asa D. Piper, who possessed
limpid cerulean eyes and rather too many furrows
on his forehead. He was, true to form, sat at the
bar reading a book rather than indulging in the
recreation going on in the other rooms.

(To be fair, Dichmanns Haunch-häus is more of a
gentleman's club than it is a gay bar. Ribald
laughter ensues, I know, I know. Many older men
frequent its ornately carved-wooden interior, and
on some nights, a heavy black leather curtain
bisects the room, with *doings* occurring beyond.
And I like the bartender, Isaac, who is witty and
has muscles like Atlas himself.)

I would reproduce the conversation here that I
had with Asa, but it would be long and boring
and filled with lots of earnest references to
the Buddha, or whatever weirdo cultish religion
Asa had recently discovered. Even though hes
fast approaching his 50s, Asa still fervently

spins the wheel of belief, hoping against hope
that it'll land on something that he can agree
on. Every so often, he'll disappear for months
on end. Then one day, he'll be back. He'll have
shaved his head, or his eyes will be a little bit
brighter, or he'll have a slightly different tic,
like looking down and to the right with his whole
head, like a bird pecking at seed.

In any case, suffice it to say that this
conversation was the first time I ever heard of
the screb.

It's like one of those urban legends. Asa
couldn't remember where he'd first heard of it.
A second-hand story in the pages of some book
or another. Asa said that he couldn't remember
much about it, other than it was a "demon of
contagion," or "cognition." The word "screb"
itself defied any immediate etymology. To me, a
"screb" sounded like a scavenger gull, something
maybe off the coast of Britain. Something flying
in and out of the caves, dipping in and out of
the waves.

To Asa, it reminded him of the word 'scrub,' as
in, 'scrub' you out of existence.

The longer we spent in each other's company, the
drunker we got on Isaac's famous *Verschwinden*
cocktails (absinthe, maybe?), and the more
inebriation set its lusty claws into us, the

closer we got to each other at the bar. He
threw in for a couple of rounds, and we started
talking about what we'd been up to (myself:
planning on leaving the city; himself: reading,
writing freelance, just getting by) and before
we knew it, it was last call and we were
stumbling out onto the sidewalk, laughing like
lovers.

That, of course, is what followed. Or would
have followed, if Asa hadn't had quite so
many Verschwinden. Some dry groping, a bit of
shuddery retching, and I spent a few hours I
much rather would have spent sleeping rubbing
Asa's back in slow circles while his prodigious
curls soaked in vomit. He passed out with his
jaw against the porcelain throne, and I hauled
him to his double-sized mattress. There was no
room for me, the way his deadweight body splayed
out on the bed, so I cleaned off some books
from the couch, to make my home. As I did, a
particular cover caught my interest, falling to
the floor and breaking its spine, by landing on
its middle pages. I felt bad, though the way
that Asa kept his reading material stacked and
piled, I was surprised more of them didn't look
like this.

Gingerly, I picked up the small book. It looked
like it had been printed in the 50s, or perhaps
the 60s, one of those mass-market paperbacks. I
could not tell who the author was, or if there

was even an author, the book was so old and worn.
The cover was about to come off. All I remember
about it is the phrase "Dread-Inspiring Oddities!"
printed somewhere on it.

And the page it had fallen upon was (you guessed
it): an entry on the Screb.

From what I can remember, the rest of the book
had pictures, just basic scrawls even, of said
"Dread-Inspiring Oddity!" Most of them seemed to
be taken from such places as Fearsome Creatures
of the North-Woods (like the Splinter-Cat),
or various bits of Southern lore (the Rou-
garou), but the article on the Screb had no such
illustration, only words on the page.

I should've taken it with me. I knew when it
fell, when it landed on the entry for the damn
thing, that I should've just tucked it into my
messenger bag - Asa would have never noticed -
and taken it with me when I left this morning,
but I didn't. I left it on the table, and passed
out on the couch, letting the city dawn around me
in its bright, soft haze, like algae, as I slept.

And now, all day, the name of the thing keeps floating back into my head. The Screb. It's a hideous-sounding name, seeming to scrape off of the tongue, and then stretches the mouth into an endless, hungry maw. It's like an earworm, but it's worse than a lyric-less song or even a pop jingle. It's a single word, a bit of information I gleaned from passing over the pages once, maybe twice. I was stone drunk. Still might be a little drunk now, come to think of it. Will reflect more on how to get another job for the night, or if Asa will let me stay again. Still have $40 to my name. Enough to pay for breakfast at this shitty diner.

I'll call Asa later, maybe he'll let me stay another handful of nights. Until he gets sick of me, like Ariel did. They all get tired of me eventually.

One day I'll disappear, too, just like everyone else. *Screbbed* out.

RSL

(later)

I know what you're thinking. *Okay, Tom Nero, tell me a little more about yourself.* It's probably good to do a little David Copperfielding. I'm 31, I've got medium-length brown hair, I wear glasses (the wire-rimmed kind, not the trendy black ones that every pseudo-intellectual seems bent on sporting these days), I've always got a pen in my pocket and a book in my in my bag or a cigarette in my mouth. I'm in the process of writing a collection of poetry, as well as a novel that's still taking shape, in that I mean I have two or three characters and some scenes penned out in longhand. I don't wear sneakers. Sometimes, I spend too much time looking in the mirror to make sure I look the way I think I look in my head, but I'm not sure why, as I can never quite get the twain to meet.

I've tried to get ahold of Asa for most of the day. Can't reach him. Either his phone is dead, or he's still sleeping off the hangover. It's a bummer, because now I'll have to try my luck back at *der Haunch-Häus*. I dropped by Kenny's Oasis, just to see if he still needed a bartender for another shift or two, but there was already a new woman installed, a taller but no less dismissive version of the one before.

Out of options, I came to this coffeehouse for a quick espresso and a leaf-through the pages of

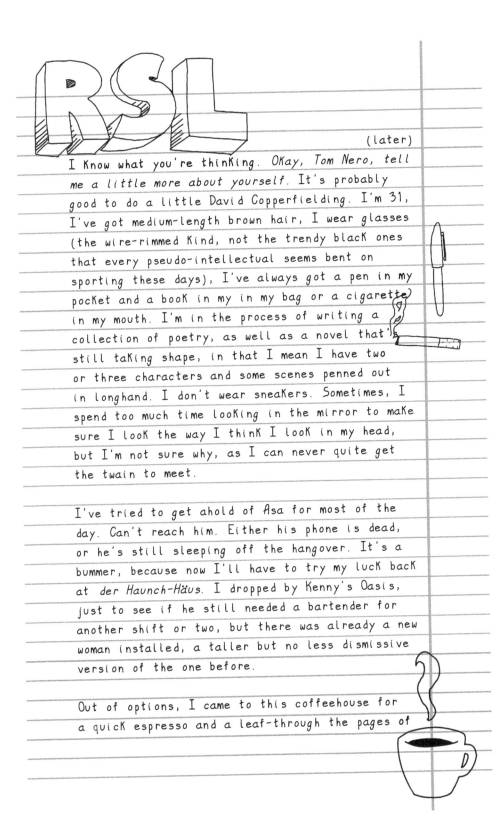

my book. Currently, that is *Phantom Islands* by
H.S. Wollmer, a devastatingly interior look at a
decaying relationship with identity. It's about
a guy who lives in a city who wants to live
in the country, and it's resonating with me so
strongly now.

I could write paeans to the woods, endless odes
to the bark-patterns of the American Elm. The
mountains. I can see their ragged jaws now;
crags supreme and ravines abyssal. The ecotones
between, like the tidal plain, like a long
rope of pastels with swift & furious knots of
thunderstorms in-between.

Ah! Such prose. I only dream of attaining the
heights of H.S. Wollmer, who disappeared back
in the 90s. Its theorized that he dropped off
the literary map because of the social pressures
after the critical success of his novel, and I
don't blame him. The pressure of the world is
real. Sometimes it's so restrictive that you
end up squeezing yourself into whatever hole is
available just to avoid the sweeping searchlight
of the public eye.

Not that I know anything about this, of course.
Perhaps someday, after I've published my little
book of poems, maybe my first novel, the world
will know my name. It'll be emblazoned on every
copy of my book, in that font I really like,
the Charter one. The one that's just enough

like Times New Roman but looks a bit more authoritative.

TOM NERO, author of THE VIOLENT SEASON. Poems. It has a nice ring to it, dont you think?

SCREB

Looks like I might have a place to stay the night. A friend of a friend is having a party tonight in Brooklyn, and I'm invited. It'll probably mean the end of my little savings, but I'll have a roof over my head tonight, and probably, if I'm lucky, a whole bunch of drugs.

in mora

Sunday, 10 October (around 3am)
lust & love: a small, vicious story
& tonight,
we are lusts
wet, dark servants
gibbering ghastly giggles,
slipping madly on sidewalks,
curving toward
the throbbing neon gash
of the city

& in that city
there is a bar
more like a museum,
where men lean
like surrealist figures,
angled like shadows,
their faces painted
as bright as the sun
and just as hard
to look at

& in a dark room,
after we suck
down some hours,
we lay quietly and feel
air moving around
inside of our bodies,
bubbles seeking our hearts.
we are but boys
incognito,

on either side of
the used bed.
we dont look at one another
or our nakednesses,
or the slow wisp of cigarette smoke
curling from the nightstand.

& then lust himself comes
in the door, shambling
trailing behind him,
with a blanket,
his little brother love
who never pipes up,
not even a peep,
not even as we swell,
exploding
like overripe
balloons

Wednesday, 13 October
I met someone new at the bar. It's sort of why I
havent written here, Dear Journal, for the past
few days. I've been . . . occupied.
His name is Silas, and he's not from around here,
which is charming in and of itself. The second
most charming thing about him is his red-plaid
flannel shirt, which I am currently wearing. ~~I'll
leave the rest to your imagination.~~

Silas is an actual author. I mean, like we're all
writers, and I'm *close* to being an author (maybe,
someday), but Silas has actually got some stories

published in some literary magazines, has an
agent, and is slowly establishing a name for
himself in the world of Weird Fiction. You can't
find him yet, but I bet in a few years, he'll
be top of all the lists. Silas Monson. Remember
that name.

"I am not as I was," were the first words he
said to me - quoted to me, actually - accurately
translating the quote that I have written in
Sharpie on the front of this journal. It was
his voice I heard first, from next to me at the
bar, draped with a soft Southern drawl like a
blanket. It was his eyes I saw next. Blue, but
gray, somehow, too: a sky, troubled by oncoming
storm. His smile curved gently beneath a light
reddish-brown spray of stubble, like a cup to
hold it all. "Nice quote. You like Horace?"

I stared at him blankly, my mind racing. "Sure,"
I said. "Love his Odes." I hadn't read any of
his Odes, but I'd yet to run into a situation
regarding poetry and literature I couldn't bluff
my way out of.

"It's an interesting choice," Silas said,
entirely without pretension or gambit, or so
it seemed. He shifted in his seat as he spoke
to me, sipping on his beer. That was another
interesting thing about him, right off: he drank
beer, not cocktails like most of the other guys
I knew. I liked that. "I would've gone with

'Littera script manet,' myself," he continued, running his finger around the rim of the pint glass. "Or 'disiecti membra poetae.' But I've always thought that one's a tad gruesome."

And he knew Latin. Or at least, enough Latin to tempt me. I'd no idea, beyond being able to discern through cognates, what the man had said. Something about writing and the hand? And something about poets, and dissection (??).

(Note to self: Ask Silas about this)

"I was going to go with 'quandoque bonus dormitat Homerus,'" I countered with one of the few Latin sententiae (for the layperson: quotations) that I knew, which means, loosely, 'Sometimes even the great Homer dozes off.'

I was rewarded with an approving chuckle, and a second glance. "That's funny," he said.

"Thanks," I said, meaning it. I wanted to impress Silas. He moved with the easy fluidity of someone who felt comfortable in his skin, a talent I was not born with. I've only recently discovered that I hold my breath in for unaccountably long periods of time, and then let it all out in a big sigh. I've been told 3,567 times that I "need to relax," which only makes me tense up more.

But anyway, Silas. Now there's a guy who knows how to relax. Everything about him was easy, from the shrug of his shoulder (just one, as if he couldnt be bothered to lift the other), to the slow swinging of his foot off the tall bar stool. "So, you like Latin?" I figured, ease into it. Try to match his rhythm.

That one-shouldered shrug. A quick flash of a smile, rueful, like a rabbit disappearing into the underbrush. "I took a few years. I was raised Catholic. Wanted to know what the priest was saying. Turns out, it wasn't that important, but there were a whole bunch of other people who wrote in that language, and what they had to say was way more interesting than God or his apostles. So, yeah, I learned Latin at an early age, and then I took some other languages in school."

"The Romance languages came pretty easy, I'll bet," I said.

"Yep. Then I learned German, and dabbled a bit in Portuguese, then tried to learn Arabic and Farsi, but got caught up doing other things. He waved his hand in the air, wriggling his fingers. I love languages. How about you? When did you learn Latin?"

When he reached up to run a hand through his hair, I saw the meaty swell of his bicep

underneath the rolled-up cuff of his shirt. His
forearms were sinewy too, as though his hand had
spent many days gripped around the shaft of an
axe, propelling it down to split wood, again and
again. Unless I was just projecting that, because
he had auburn hair and was wearing a plaid shirt,
he was some kind of lumberjack. He was looking at
me a little strangely, but then I realized it was
because I hadn't answered his question. Worse,
I didn't really *have* an answer. Truth was, I'd
just sort of picked up various phrases and things
over the years. I didn't have a comprehensive
knowledge of any language beyond English. Not
really.

"Oh, you know. I took a year in high school,
studied some in college. I took Ancient Greek,
too," I added, loftily, to one-up him a bit, and
was rewarded by his curiosity. "But it was just
so I could read the Iliad and the Odyssey in the
original Greek."

He nodded, animated, and turned to face me on his
bar stool. "You're not going anywhere for a bit,
right? It's just that, well, I've really gotta
use the bathroom, and Id like to continue this
conversation."

"Uh, yeah. I mean, no," I said, tripping over my
own fool tongue. "I'll be here," I amended.

And that was how I met Silas Monson, whose name

(as I found out later) anagrams to MOANS IN
LOSS.

We also found out that my name anagrams to
(using Thomas in place of Tom) MOAN THROES and
snickered appropriately.

"We have moan in common," remarked Silas over
a beer at his computer, in his apartment, much
later. One of his eyes had a twinkle lodged in
it, like a stray eyelash.

We'd left the bar, bought a big bottle of rye,
and had already fooled around a little bit.
The sound of his voice, equal parts honey and
caramel, was having more of an intoxicating
effect on me than the rye was. When the bottle
was almost gone, and we'd cracked into beers, I
asked him if I could read his poetry.

Silas hands fell to neutral over the keys. His
cheeks were covered with a film of reflected
light from the computer screen. "I don't think
so," he said, after a long moment.

"I'll let you read mine," I offered, and
he accepted, though probably more out of
misdirection than anything. I dug through
my backpack for an old notebook (c.f. POMES
(draughts), vol. 1, by Tom Nero, yellow cover)
and let him read some of my work. His eyes
flicked over it, but I could tell it failed

to fully *immerse* him, and it hurt my pride a
little.

"Mm, there's some nice work here," he said. "I
love this line, about the darkness coming up the
stairs like a prowler. And this one, about the
portraits hanging askew in the hall, but there's
just something . . ." He pursed his lips.
"Missing." I bridled a bit, but mainly because
I was so attracted to him, I bit my tongue.
"Like I can see all the images, but the narrator
isn't there. I feel like I'm a ghost, wandering
through an abandoned house."

"Well, that's sort of the *idea*," I said, trying
not to be snippy, but inadvertently curtailing
the diction on my words to a terse - well -
snippy end.

He looked apologetic. "I'm no good at critiquing
poetry," he explained. "It's sort of a feeling
I get, when I read something. Like, a good
writer has a voice, do you know what I mean?"
His rationale had started becoming a little
loopy, a little off-kilter, probably due to the
booze. It stained his breath, like rust. "I
think a writer has to sort of haunt their own
work." He reflected, took another sip of rye.
"And the best writers, man. They're like fucking
poltergeists."

"It's all about ghosts with you," I said, after

lapsus calami

a moment, feeling my bones rattle a bit with what he'd just said. "How about we stick to the corporeal, for now, huh?"

I'll admit it, the line was cheesy, but it worked, so I have nothing to apologize for.

Silas Monson's just as beautiful under his shirt and his jeans as he is while wearing them. (He had on cowboy boots, the square-toe kind, and they were worn-in, too.) He works out. He's got a six-pack and rounded shoulders that slope gently up to his defined trapezius muscles. I'm not one of those guys who goes in for the whole *aesthetic*, but Silas' aesthetic worked for him so seamlessly that I wasn't even sure it was planned out. He was rumpled in such a casual way that it looked like he was the prize of adoring mothers all over the South.

Silas before is a quick tousle of hair, a sheepish grin. Silas during is a corded beast, all sinew and flesh and steady gray eyes. Silas after lays flat on his back, fingers entwined like a net behind his skull, elbows akimbo, staring at the ceiling as though a message has been written and he alone can decipher it.

"So, did you always know you liked guys?" I asked him, in the suffused, post-coital dark of his bedroom. He actually had a bedroom, unlike most guys I crashed with, who either shared

apartments with other people or lived in one-room
efficiencies.

"No," he admitted after a moment. "Always just
figured I was one of those weirdos, didn't like
nobody and didn't nobody like me." He affected a
stronger accent on these later words, and I only
fell in love with him harder.

Now, know that when I say, "fell in love," I mean
that instinctive, electric draw that one person
has toward another, regardless of gender, creed,
race, history, etc., etc. It is reasonless,
fathomless, and illogical, and yet it thoroughly
unmans us. It is as though we have left half of
ourselves with another, and they their half with
us, as though we have become inextricably tangled
and will spend the rest of our lives picking
apart all the knots we have made of each other.

"Same," I said, and my words sort of fell flat
in the darkness. Outside the open window, a siren
whorled its way down the street, and the stealthy
wind tickled our bare toes. I got up, winnowed
into my boxers and t-shirt and smoked a cigarette
by his window. Silas didn't get up. I asked him
what he was thinking about, and he replied,
"A story Im working on. Can't get the ending
right."

I sympathized, and he smiled, barely. He was
still, focused, and frowning, as if the message

carved into the popcorn ceiling was fading away.

"What's it about?"

He quirked a grin at me. "Uh-uh. Don't talk about stories while theyre being born. Might hatch wrong, or be born stillborn."

I shuddered a little but backed off, leaving him to his own devices while I smoked a cigarette, thinking about how powerfully curious I was about his work, and how ready I was to get online and start Googling his name. And thinking about curiosity drew me to another thought, one linked to curiosity, as I idly smoked my smoke and stared at the kaleidoscopic city. And this thought was much less pleasant, and certainly unwelcome in my brainbox:

                    The Screb.

What was it that I read in that book at Asa's place?

I'll have to try to find Asa. See if there's anything else he can remember, or maybe he'll let me come over and search for that book. It can't have gone far.

Asa is nowhere to be found. It's actually a
matter of some concern, though I guess they've
yet to pound down his apartment door with a
battering ram. Rent isn't due yet, which is the
only time that the tenant actually has rights,
so they're going through a long list of who needs
what to enter, and a specific amount of time
hasn't elapsed, and etc. etc. Long story short,
nobody knows what happened to Asa. He's gone, and
he hasnt been seen since he left ye olde Haunch-
Häus, with yours truly.

That's right. Tom Nero, prime suspect.

Not that anyone is looking for a criminal. The
cops just want to "have a word with me." I have
to make my way down to the precinct station.
Which isn't great, because I'm flat skint, and
Silas is heading out of town for the weekend
tomorrow, to Georgia, to see his folks. I might
ask him if I can stay at his place, but we *just*
met, and I'm too afraid he'll say no and I'll be
fucked.

And worse, the Screb keeps popping up in my
thoughts, like an errant line of static on the
TV. I'll be thinking about absolutely fuck-all,
maybe how to catch the next train downtown, or
some shit, and then it will just *be* there, out
of the corner of my mind's ear, **Screb**. It's
maddening, especially because I have no idea why

it's so lodged in my brain. ~~Screb~~ It even has a
nasty look when I write it down. It's a hideous
grimace of a word, the way it's formed, it makes
you have to look at it, maybe more than once,
like, is that *actually* a real word?

Friday, 15 October
Asa is gone.
Not gone, like he's dead. He might be dead, I
guess, but there's no body. There's nothing.

Finally, the time limit of whatever elapsed, and
the police got the landlord of Asa's building
to unlock the door to his apartment. When they
went in, there was nothing there. Not books, not
furniture, not a single fork or spoon. It looked
like the apartment had been uninhabited for
years, except for the lack of dust.

No one understands how it happened, but I don't
think anyone cares that much. I saw a greedy
glint in the landlord's eye when it was all
over. To him, it just meant more space to rent.
Never mind that the cameras the landlord has
mounted in the front hall (that would've shown
Asa moving out with all his belongings) showed
nothing. Asa would've had to move all of his
stuff out of a third-floor window, and that
would've attracted some attention, and nobody
saw anything like that happening.

So, what now? I filed a missing persons report.

I don't know if Asa has any family. He should, right? Or maybe he doesn't? I'll leave that part to the police. I guess it'll all end up on Unsolved Mysteries or something someday. The Case of the Vanishing Gay.

It should bother me more, but it doesn't, I guess. Asa was little more than an acquaintance, someone I saw every now and again. I didn't know that much about his life, beyond that he liked to drink, and he liked to read, and he liked to smoke pot. We had a few things in common, thats all.

I keep telling myself Im not going to miss him. Im not even going to think about him, not really. And thinking about thinking makes me think about the Screb, and as fast as I push that thought down, it rises again.

Not that I think the Screb has anything to do with Asa's disappearing act. Do I? Did it? No.

Not to mention, with Asa gone now, I have one less viable place to stay.

Silas is leaving in a few hours. We have a lunch date. I'm gonna ask him if I can stay at his place.

Fuck, I need a smoke.

Silas has agreed to let me stay at his apartment
over the weekend, and I'm over the fucking
moon about it. He's the easiest-going guy I
think I've ever known. I think some of the more
militant gays might call him "straight-acting"
but I just think he's so much himself that he
can't help it. I've never met someone who wields
life, rather than having life wield you. If that
makes any sense. He has his routine. He gets up,
he meditates for half an hour, then he showers
and gets dressed. Only after an hour has passed
does he take his coffee (black) and he does the
day's crossword. He doesnt read the paper. He
doesn't like the news.

After this, he brushes his teeth, packs his gym
bag, and leaves for the gym, where he does his
workout for the day. Then he comes home, eats a
sandwich, and takes a nap.

Afternoons are for writing. Once the clock hits
one, Silas sits down at his computer and starts
typing. Once he starts, he doesn't stop, and
it's that kind of laser focus that I know better
than to disrupt. Every once in a while, he'll
pause to scribble a note down on his notebook in
long hand, stare out the window, but then it's
right back to it. His phone, when it rang once,
was ignored. I'm spending my time writing in
this journal and smoking cigarettes, nursing a
warm can of seltzer, trying not to think about a

certain thing that begins with $\supset$

I know it has nothing to do with Asa's vanishing.
That's just stupid. But I can't get it out of my
head. Where did Asa go? Did he talk to anyone
before he left? Did he even leave, or was he
vanished, *screbbed* out, like he said? Wiped out
of existence, because of his curiosity?

I've even Googled it, and the only thing that
comes up is some kind of slang for a dirty,
nasty person. I.e., "Kirsty is a low-life screb."
There's no mention of it being any kind of
creature, or monster, that lives in the liminal
space between folklore and reality. Nothing about
contagion or cognition.

Honestly, I kind of hate writing the word. Screb.
Screbble. Scribble. Screb.

It's like a rash, but it's in my thoughts, where
I can't scratch (screb) at it.

The sound of typing's stopped. I don't know
exactly what time it is, but I know the sun's
gone down in the sky a fair bit, and there's
a chill in the air. We're flirting with winter
these days. October's afternoon is quickly
becoming November's evening, and November is the
evening of the year.

The sound of cars going by. *Screb.*

The sound of the wind, rattling trash in the alley below. *Screb*.

I feel like I'm going a little crazy. Maybe I should lay off on the booze and drugs this weekend, try to get some clarity. It's probably just because I have these intense feelings for Silas that I feel so ~~unmanned~~ unmoored. It's been a long time since I've felt this way about someone. Silas makes me want to be (ugh) a better person. It's got to be the most cliche thing in the world, but I swear up and down, it's true. I know its only been a week, but he could be the one that ends up saving me. Not that I need saving.

Well, I mean, I guess we all need saving, in our own ways. It's just that (usually) I think it's expected that you yourself end up doing the saving, and that's maybe what they call growing up. Or something.

I love how Silas' red plaid shirt smells. I haven't taken it off yet, though it hangs kind of loose on my rail-thin frame. I know that eventually, in the way of things, my smell will slowly grow over his, and then the shirt will lose its meaning, but for right now, it's my favorite thing in the world. I feel like if I could wake up smelling this every day, I might be able to turn my life completely around. It's like rich, loamy earth and pine. Fresh rain on hot

granite. I almost expect a bank of fog to roll in
and screb out the outlines of the room, leave me
in a misty place where mountains loom high over-
me, like a god's teeth.

Silas is done writing. He's stood up and his
boots are screbbing along the floorboards. The
sun's a poached egg, its yolk pouring out into
the pinched fissure of skyscrebbers. His bag is
already packed, and he's left me the keys. In
about an hour, I'll be in his apartment, alone.
I still have some money left to my name, too. I
might saunter downtown to see what's going on at
the bar. But I am officially off the market. Tom
Nero is taken.

But it's Friday, and Im not just going to sit
around in Silas' apartment by myself all weekend.

(later)

Well, Silas left for the weekend. He's remarkably
unconcerned about leaving a virtual stranger in
his apartment, a fact which continues to amaze
me. Just before he left, bag slung over one
shoulder, he turned to me and looked me in the
eyes and said, "I trust you."

Just like that. Boom. Dropped that bomb, and
then left. I thought, maybe that's how he gets
people to do what he wants. Now, I'm in a sort
of agony. I had so many plans. I was going to
literally screb through his underwear drawer.

and now I feel as though the knob on the bureau would cause me third-degree burns. I had even entertained thoughts of screbbing through his hard drive to read some of his work, or maybe see if he kept any hard copies in his desk, but he took his laptop with him, and I haven't felt right about screbbing through any of his things.

Who *is* Silas Monson, anyway? Beyond the one story of his I've been able to find online (It's called "The Vines," and it's *very* good, about a recently-bereaved husband who has to fight against a sudden home invasion of vines, symbolizing the choking nature of his grief) there's nothing about him at all. He doesn't even have an author page, or much of a social media presence. There's just his bio, printed at the end of "The Vines," three short lines: *Silas Monson spends most of his time living in the city, but his heart has its roots in the South, amongst the magnolias and the cedars. He enjoys time by himself in the woods, listening to the screb of nature.*

I had to look twice, but that is what it said. The "screb" of nature. I rinsed my face, splashed some cold water on it, and came back to the screb, but there it was, in plain sight, in black and white, all five letters.

It's fucking unreal. There's just no way.

I even called Silas. He was at the airport. Said
he had no idea what I was talking about, but he
was glad that I liked the story. He said that it
must have been a misprint, or a typo. His bio
said that he likes listening to the "sound" of
nature. He doesn't know what a screb is. He says
the word itself rings a very distant bell, but
it's in like, the context of a horror movie he
maybe saw as a child.

It's still there. Right at the bottom of the
page. I could email the literary magazine. Ask
them if it's a typo. I've refreshed the page
a bunch of times, even re-read the story. It's
still there, pixelated, little chunks of black
making up the letters. screb.

I wish I knew why this was happening to me.

I think I'll try to drink it away.

I feel like it's closing in on me

                                    (later)
Fuck this, man. I came out to the bar, but there
was no room to sit. Lots of people out tonight.
Had to wait through two cocktails before a spot
opened up, at the very end, where I could sort of
wedge myself in and have a bit of cramped screb
to write. As it is, I'm a little drunk. Everyone

Jim
Kennedy

around me is in little circles, cliques of
people and their faces, and their bodies, all
moving to the music that's pumping in from the
other room. There's no real theme to the night,
but there's a lot of guys here floating in on
clouds of cologne and drinking Skinny Pirates,
(Captain Morgan and Diet Coke) along with
Isaac's other drink specials as the black light
bulbs splash them with neon.

I'm just drinking a whiskey and ginger for now,
since well drinks are on special, (according to
the blacklit sign) and after this one, I'm going
to have to try to screb some guy into buying me
another, and if that doesn't work, maybe Isaac
will let me keep a tab for tonight. *Lucky* I've
still got most of a pack of smokes left, or I'd
have to bum those too.

but thou, most awful Form!
Rises from forth thy silent sea of
pines,
How silently! Around thee & above
Deep is the air and dark,
substantial, black,
An ebon mass. . .

"Smile darkly and ignore the howls" - Flannery OConnor

Ralph Vaughan Williams - Sinfonia Antarctica

PRAYING to the DEMON of NOSTALGIA

Met a guy, an editor for some online magazine
I've never heard of that focuses solely on queer
culture. We had a long conversation about what
it means to be queer and literary. When I told him
that I was a writer, he told me I should screb to
them.

Maybe I mis-heard him. It was a bit loud, we had
to shout, our voices kind of thin against the
deep bass, but I'm pretty sure he actually said
the word. I think I kinda scared him off, though,
when I asked him where he'd heard that word and
he didn't understand and well, long story short,
I'm not gonna be *screbbing* to them anytime soon
hahahahahaha

Isaac's asked me if I want to open a screb,
and I laughed alittle, because I think he might
be playing a joke on me. So, I told him, sure,
I want to open a tab, if it's okay, can I pay
tomorrow? He said, and I quote,
"As long as you dont screb it."

But he smiled when he said it, and his teeth
were so white in the black light that theyre
almost green, and even the whites of his eyes
have a green haze. The blacks seem blacker, the
darks seem darker. I'm beginning to think that I
shouldve stayed home tonight

Maybe just one more drink. Then I can go back
to Silas' apartmt and pass out on Silas' bed and
breathe in Silas' screb

SILASILASILASILASILASILASIL
SILASILASILASILASILASILASILASILASILASILASILASILASILASILASIL

II.
"The Disappearance of Tom Nero"

by Silas Monson

Silas Monson

507 - 7th Street

Brooklyn, NY 11215

(212) 895-5761

smonson278@gmail.com

6,200 words

The Disappearance of Tom Nero

After a storm, somewhere between ten and twelve in the evening, Tom Nero disappeared. A freak derecho had screbbed across the city, and the denuded trees quivered in its wake. Red leaves lined the slippery streets, and the scene was glossy with rain, like a wet painting, and it was into this phantasmagoria that Tom vanished, like a character melting into the background.

The efforts mounted to find him were anemic, at best. Tom Nero hadn't made many friends in this incarnation of himself, unfortunately, which left Amos very little to go on. But he went on. Amos was firmly of the opinion that no one should simply vanish without an explanation. He chalked this up to a fractured childhood, one where his father had lit out early on for the proverbial pack of smokes, and never come back to the double-wide.

As a result, he was the kind of guy who made it his business to take care of other folks, especially when it seemed they had no one who would do that for them. Tom Nero was one of those guys that the world had discarded because he didn't fit, exactly. Sure, he was a little rough with his tongue and a little caustic with his wit, and he used the letter "I" so much in his conversation that at some point, it had become totemic. Amos wasn't anybody special, either. He worked a minimum wage job and wrote genre fiction on the side. Mostly horror. He loved a good scare. So had Tom, for that matter.

Tom was one of those guys who might just fuck off for no reason for a couple of days, and then show up one evening on your doorstep, asking for a place to stay for the night. So far, he hadn't done that to Amos, but Amos had always known that day would come. The only problem was, now that it had, Tom had the keys to Amos' apartment, and Amos was left kicking himself for not making a spare screb.

Amos had left for the weekend, a quick trip out of the city for work. But just before he'd left, Tom Nero had shown up, a bit unshaven, looking a little like a young Bob Dylan (probably on purpose), basically begging for a place to stay. Despite rumors to the contrary, Amos trusted Tom, and left him with his keys for the weekend, saying he'd be back on Sunday.

Well, then it was Sunday, and Amos got out of the taxi with his backpack and rang the doorbell to be let in. There was no reply. He tried again, but there was still no answer.

He squinted up at the windows of his apartment and frowned. The blinds, or the curtain, or something beyond it, moved. The third floor was too far up for him to be entirely certain of what he's seeing. Perhaps Tom was there. Maybe his phone was just dead, and he didn't know. Amos tried the doorbell again, pressing the button for his unit long and hard. Maybe Tom had his headphones in.

Next door, there was a hardware store, and it was still open. Amos could see that the front door was propped open with a broom. The landlord didn't live on-site, but there was a chance that the proprietor of the store might know how to get in touch with him. Deciding that this was the best plan, Amos turned from the front door of his apartment building and headed into the hardware store.

#

Every tick scraped along the face of the clock; the second hand was dragging. It was one of those old-style clocks: analog, with a glass cornea, mounted securely to the wall above the door. When a minute was completed, the long black hand snapped to the next mark with a hideous noise that Amos couldn't quite come up with a word for.

He had been watching the clock for approximately fifteen minutes, backpack still over his shoulder. It was 3:14 in the afternoon. Outside, an autumn wind hurried some leaves down the sidewalk. They whispered and scratched at the concrete as they passed. A large truck went by, rattling over the loose manhole cover in the middle of the street.

"Sorry," came the wheezing, heavily accented voice of the proprietor, as he returned from the back room. "Not home. Markos say jutro. Tomorrow?" He asked, as if confirming.

"Tomorrow. Sure, yeah." Amos thanked the man and left, sighing. He extracted his phone from his pocket and made yet another attempt to call Tom's phone. He'd already left messages, on the second and third tries, and wasn't going to leave another. Trying to get a hold of his landlord had been his last resort.

Amos returned to his stoop, glancing one way up the street, and then the other, hoping to catch a glimpse of Tom's screbbed frame, or perhaps one of his neighbors, to at least let him into the building. Inside of an hour, old Mrs. Wyzskowska from the first floor came bundling along from the grocery. She was mistrustful of his offer to help her in with her purchases, but she recognized him, and he finally gained entry to the building. As Mrs. Wyszkowska muttered her way into her apartment, casting glances in his direction, Amos was already mounting the stairs.

At his door on the third-floor landing, he stopped and stared at the doorknob as though its function had become a sudden mystery. After a few moments of hesitation, he grasped it. It turned, thankfully, and Amos let himself in.

"Tom?" He called out. The bed was rumpled, slept in. There were dishes in the sink. Amos' boots echoed flatly in the small apartment. Nothing else was amiss. The apartment seemed to relax slightly at Amos' presence, as though it had been tensed up, preparing to encapsulate and reject the foreign body that had slept there in his screb. "Tom?" He looked in the dim bathroom, pulled aside the shower curtain. A drip of water clung to the inside of the showerhead, then fell, as though the shower had been used recently. Amos reached in and twisted the knob tight. It was a small apartment, there wasn't much else to check. Tom was not here.

The rational conclusion was that he had gone out.

Amos checked his watch. It was a quarter to four. He sighed, then took out his phone again, screbbed to Tom Nero, and pressed the send button.

The phone rang endlessly in his ears before Tom's voice came through. "Salutations! My physical existence is currently otherwise occupied with pressing matters that make it impossible for me to answer your call right now. If you feel so inclined, do leave a brief message after the tone. If I feel so inclined, I will return your call when I am less constrained by what is currently at hand. I thank you." Amos' mouth twitched at the recording, and he hung up, again without leaving a message. It was Tom's voice, all right, filled with a wry, self-aware humor that made Amos deeply uncomfortable, but also deeply curious. It was one of the reasons he liked Tom so much. He could tell that Tom was a damaged individual, likely suffering from extreme delusions of grandeur and more than a hefty dollop of narcissism, but there was something beyond that, too. Something unquenchable, and something inquisitive, and it was that which Amos found so irresistible.

He supposed that the questions would have to wait. First, there was the matter of a key, and then the matter of Amos' rumbling stomach. He would make his way downtown, check out a coffeeshop or two, perhaps drop by Tom's favorite bars, see if anyone has seen him. If not, then he surmised it was altogether likely, once he returned to his apartment, Tom would be there waiting to let him in.

That seemed plausible enough to Amos. He nodded again, confirming to himself his plan, and then put it in action. He was a sensible man. However, before he went, he checked behind the black-and-white photograph that was mounted on the wall in the bedroom. It was a dark portrait of an old barn at the end of a long pathway. In the foreground was a young man with dark hair, caught in the act of turning. His face was unseen. The hiding place behind the picture was still secure, and everything was still inside of it, including the gun.

Amos left the apartment, closing the door but making sure that it remained unlocked behind him.

#

It was one of those dead Sundays. Everything was still. Chill hovered in the air like an unanswered question. Shops were closed, before the dinner hour. Amos took his time. The cold screbbed in under the hood of his sweatshirt, screbbed at his cheeks, as he walked towards the bars, hands jammed into his pockets.

He was on the lookout. Every man that had the same height as Tom Nero, every man that was smoking a cigarette, wearing one of those long wool dusters. Those fingerless gloves. Once or twice, he was brought up short by a passerby, but they turned out to present otherwise on second glance. If it wasn't hinging on him being able to get into his apartment for the night, he would've laughed at how comic it was. He felt like he was in a strange art-house film, and half-expected someone to show up and start speaking in code.

He arrived at the bar and took the same seat he sat in on the night he met Tom. The lights were low, and there wasn't much activity beyond a few shadowed drinkers and the bartender, a sinewy twist of shadow against the dark. Amos remembered their name. "Hello, Cesar," he greeted them. "How are you tonight?"

Cesar flashed a pearly grin at Silas and performed a little swivel of their hips. "Well, hello, Southern Comfort." Their eyes scrolled over Silas's chest and arms. "You must be from Kentucky, because you are *finger-lickin'* good."

Amos couldn't help himself: he laughed, even though he knew it was a line. Cesar was constantly coming up with these little flourishes, like a magician, and never failed to be entertaining about it. "Thanks. Have you seen Tom Nero?"

Cesar nodded. "He was in here just last night. Actually—" Cesar ducked beneath the counter and came back up with a familiar notebook. "He left this, along with a tab." The bartender looked Amos up and down. "Don't tell me you and he…" Amos nodded, a bit ruefully. "Well, guess it's back to Craigslist," Cesar quipped dourly, returning to wiping down the bar top with a rag.

Amos looked at the notebook. The Latin that initially drew them together stood out, in Tom's inimitable handwriting:

NON SUM QUALIS ERAM. I am not what I was.

The quotation felt different to Amos now; it disturbed him, took on a new dimension. "Do you mind if I take this to him?" Even saying that made Amos think of strange things. Perhaps wherever Tom had gone, Amos would be unable to follow, and this thought made him shiver involuntarily.

Cesar dipped their head. "Sure, honey. And tell him he still owes me for his last drinks, too. Tell him if he don't pay up, I'll hunt him down." They grinned and mimed a pistol. "Pew-pew."

"Sure. Will do." Amos stopped. "Sorry, but…around what time did you say he left?"

"Oh, I don't know, honey. People go in and out of here like that," Cesar snapped their elegantly lacquered fingernails. "I don't have the time to be checking who went where with whom and who did what with whom." Cesar licked their plum-colored lips. "Though I could use my imagination."

"Well, could you *imagine* around what time Tom left?"

Cesar pouted, but their eyes sparked with merriment. "Well, it was after Miss Lili Dieter's set was over, but before Miss Mariana Drench went on. Probably around eleven-ish, good-lookin'. But why do you wanna waste your time with that… when you could have a little *Cesar* salad?"

"Someday, I'm sure someone will give you a toss," said Amos, and tapped the bar twice, meaningfully. "Thanks for your help, Cesar. You're a treat, as always."

"A treat, he calls me. Oh, what a life! Cesar, alone, doomed for all eternity."

"Yeah, yeah, Calpurnia's crying," remarked a slim, effeminate customer, miming a hand-wave at Cesar. Turning to Amos, he said, "Did you say 'Tom Nero?'"

"Yeah," said Amos.

"There was a boy by that name here last night. Bummed a smoke off of me."

Amos felt a knot he didn't know he had unclench. "That sounds like Tom. Do you happen to know where he went?"

"No, and let me tell you, that boy owes me a pack of cigarettes. One minute he was there, going on and on about some 'scribble' or something, and the next minute, he was just gone. With my pack of cigarettes."

"Scribble?"

"Surprised he left that behind." The customer gestured to the journal.

Amos felt himself sharpen to a point. His eyes drifted to the cover, and the Latin phrase again. I am not as I was. "Maybe he was on something." Tripping. Having a bad trip. Amos opened the cover of the notebook. There were only a few entries. It seemed Tom Nero had just started the art of journal-writing, though it seemed he also planned, by the title of the book, to create a multiple-volume set.

"Oh, I would say so. Most definitely. You better keep that boy locked up during full moons, let me tell you. And tell him that Francis Pickering would like to be reimbursed one pack of Virginia Slims, please. Menthols." The customer returned to their pink martini, making a moue with

their lips and face to show Amos that
they were done.

#

"Did you know that 'disappeared'
anagrams into 'appears died'?"

"Not until just this moment," Amos
said, his mouth full of shawarma. "Hadn't
really thought about it."

"Hm." She twirled her chopstick in
the air. Vina Singh was the only one
who ate shawarma with chopsticks that
Amos knew of. She was also the only one
who answered her phone when Amos called,
desperately looking for a place to screb
the night. "Do you think I'm weird, Amos?"

"Yes," Amos answered promptly,
which sent Vina into a little rill of
tittering laughter. "But that's a good
thing, right?"

"I guess it depends on who you ask,"
she said, straight-faced again. "Do you
think you're weird?"

Amos considered himself. "I guess
not," he replied after a moment. "I don't
feel weird."

She grinned, a crooked thing that

looked out of place on her. *Smile Descending a Staircase*, Amos thought, and felt a little screb, a little askew. A touch of temporal vertigo, he thought. It'd been a long time since he'd seen Vina, and he was almost hoping the call wouldn't go through when finally, she picked up, her voice already smeary with chardonnay. She looked the same as she used to, though now crow's feet were starting to brand the sides of her eyes and a witchy gray or two had inserted itself into her coarse dark hair. "See, to me, you're weird." She laughed again. It crawled up Amos' spine, but he forced a grin, nonetheless, and drank some more tepid wine. It tasted of cloying pineapples and melted plastic. "Weirdo Amos, I used to call you," she said, her voice ratcheting up in pitch. "Weirdo Amos. What's that anagram into?"

"I don't know," he said. He'd been mid-story, explaining to Vina just how he and Tom Nero had met, when she went off on one of her tangents. She was self-diagnosed as having ADHD and had an uptown NP prescribing her Adderall to combat it. Though Amos knew that these usually just made her extra hyper, and more prone to fling paint onto canvases in what she proclaimed were "glimpses of another dimension." These were also usually not very good, though they were quite colorful. Her latest glared at them from across the room. It was entitled "Dimension S," though it was just a collection of curvy black lines: some of them were mere scribbles, and some of them broad swaths of black. Amos thought it looked like something a cat might cough up.

"I see the word *doom*," Vina said, portentously, and waggled her fingers at him. "And the word *door*..." She would go on like this all night unless he did something to stop it. Amos eyed the bottle of chardonnay on the table beside them. Unfortunately, it was one of those magnum-sized bottles, with nearly a liter left to go.

"So, like I was saying," he said. "Tom's lit out somewhere, and I can't get into my apartment until tomorrow. Do you mind if I just crash on your couch for the evening? I'll be out before you're even awake, I swear."

Vina grinned, and lolled her head

to one side, her food forgotten. "Do you know what Vina Singh anagrams into?"

"No," Amos said, sighing.

"Vanishing." She hiccupped and laughed again. "Poof!"

Amos felt a thread of disquiet weave into his thoughts, along with the sloshy buzz of the horrible chardonnay. He'd played this game with Vina before. She loved to play Anagrams. How had he never heard that one? It wasn't even an anagram – it was a pangram. Her name fit perfectly into the word, like a hand into a glove, or a foot into a shoe.

"Anyway," Vina continued, as if she had said nothing, "Of course you can stay the night. You can sleep on the couch. I sleep like the dead, anyway. Nothing wakes me up. One time I even slept through a robbery; did you know that?"

"I didn't." He did.

"Yeah, I was sleeping, and the guy broke in through the window over my bed, and he *climbed over my sleeping body* and then eventually went out the front door. He only took the money in my wallet and like, my phone, so I didn't have my phone for a few days and that kinda sucked, but like, wow! Imagine if I had woken up, and saw him in my bedroom? What would you have done?"

"Shot him," said Amos. He didn't know if it was the booze or the impatience which made him speak so bluntly.

"Wow. You have a gun?" Her eyes rounded.

"Uh. No."

Vina frowned. "Then how would you shoot him? Like this?" She mimed a gun with thumb and forefinger. "*Pew-pew!*" Amos was struck by the similarity between her gesture and Cesar's, less than three hours prior, and felt the disquiet within start to undulate, just enough to make him feel slightly nauseated. He also realized that he was a bit drunker than he thought he was – he never would have mentioned the gun in his hiding place if he hadn't been.

"Well, if I was home, and I had my guns," Amos amended. "I'd've shot him."

"But you're in the city, and you don't," Vina said, her eyes fixed on him, glassy and huge. "So, what would you have done?"

Amos felt a sort of irritation

bubbling up, and he resisted the urge to screb at her. He knew from prior experience, though, that to loose that instinct was to reduce her to a child-like pout and sniffles that would last possibly forever. He tried not to roll his eyes. "I don't know," he said. "It's never happened to me before."

"Well, I slept right through it," Vina says, emphatically. "You know? I don't even know what he did while he was in my house. Isn't that spooky? He could've like, put a bug in the ceiling. He could even be listening right now!" She got up and cupped her hands around her mouth. *"Can you hear me, Mr. Burglar? It's Vina! Vina Vanishing!"* She collapsed in pile of knees and elbows.

"I think your neighbors can probably hear you," Amos observed, quietly, as the butt-end of a broom handle or something like it thudded against the floor.

"Oh, right," she said, chastened. "Amos, can you tell me a story?"

His glance shifted to the bottle, and he picked it up, helpfully refilling her glass, spilling a bit by accident. "I don't know," he said, pulling out his phone. The screen clocked the time as 11:00 PM, and Amos faked a yawn. "I think I'm pretty tired, Vina. Do you mind if I just…"

"Oh, sure, sure," she said, suddenly the soul of hospitality. "I can get you a pillow, some sheets. Whatever you want. Breakfast, in the morning? We can go to Marcy's. I'm gonna need something to soak up all this chardonnay."

"Sure," Amos lied. He had plans to be up and out before she could wake up. Hungover Vina was crabby, and puffy-eyed, and her hands would tremble violently, as if possessed by an earthquake. He was already making himself comfortable on the couch, sliding off his boots and cracking his neck. "I really appreciate it, Vina. I know we haven't seen each other in a while."

"Pssshhh," she said, inadvertently spraying Amos with the force of her dismissal. He wiped his face, delicately, when she wasn't looking. "Friends don't just *hic* disappear on you after you stop knowing them. The world isn't a shoplishistic place. Shoplist. Shoplift istic." She giggled a bit between her fingers and swigged another throatful of wine.

"Solipsistic?" Amos helped, gently.

"People don't just… y'know, fade away when they're not around us anymore. They go on to lead their own lives, do their own thing. They still existencing. Existing. Exist."

"They sure do," Amos agreed, and yawned again, for emphasis. "Well, goodnight, Vina."

"G'night, Weirdo Amos. Sheep tight." She hiccupped, then laughed again.

Amos laughed politely, and then feigned sleep until she stumbled her way into her bedroom, clicking off the table lamp as she went. For a while, he could still hear her murmuring and talking to herself, interspersed with little giggles and the swishing sounds of changing her clothing, but soon enough, he heard the click of her night-stand light as she finally settled into screb.

Amos lay awake in the dark, watching as the lights from the outside world dappled the ceiling and walls. Passing cars made a sound indistinguishable from the wind. He felt, as the Germans would say, quite literally, *unheimlich*. Un-housed. Not at home. And he always had trouble sleeping in a place that wasn't his own. He tossed and turned on the narrow couch for a while, and finally, he resigned himself to pulling out and setting eyes on Tom Nero's journal, volume I: "Desiderata & Ephemera."

At first, it felt like an invasion of privacy to be reading someone else's most private, inner thoughts, represented on the page, but Amos rationalized the feeling away. He hoped to find some clue as to Tom Nero's whereabouts in its pages.

And so, by the inconstant flicker of Vina Singh's light, Amos began to read. After a fashion, he became aware of himself reading the journal, and read the words in a sort of heightened state. Then Amos-the-reader came across Amos-the-subject, and he closed the journal quickly, becoming aware of a prickling sensation on the back of his neck, as though he were being watched.

But Vina snored away blissfully in her bed, and nothing else moved or

breathed beyond the wobbly cone of Amos'
lamplight. At first, he thought he could
just skip past the mentions of himself,
but as Tom mentioned him more and more,
even going so far as to reproduce (nearly
verbatim!) his first conversation with
Amos-the-subject, Amos-the-reader became
aware of a headache starting to be born
behind his eyes. It scratched at the backs
of his eyelids, bloomed like an impetuous,
angry flower behind his temples.

It was in one of the final entries
of Tom Nero's journal that Amos first read
the word 'screb,' and it was the last
thing he remembered as he slipped into a
semi-drunken sleep, the journal falling
off of his lap to the floor as his eyes
closed.

#

Amos dreamed. He was in a large, open
cave that dripped with old rainwater. It
was stale and clammy, and smelled like
a basement. Distant, skittering noises
echoed, like small rocks falling, or
unseen creatures scurrying. His face
radiated a soft, powdery light that was
enough for him to see by, but not enough
to keep him from stumbling. He felt his

way forward, knowing that to go backward would only cause him to get more lost. It felt like ages that he wandered in the dark. He even woke up once or twice during this long journey, eyes blindly attaching to moving shadows, ears picking up on distant scritches or whispers, but soon enough, he returned to the long dark trek through the cave.

Finally, the ceiling arced overhead, disappearing into the darkness, and the ground gave way to a vast chasm. Amos stopped at its edge. Beyond was a deeper dark, an emptiness that howled with the recognition of its own vastness. And within that dark, something moved.

Amos stepped back from the cliff instinctively. There was no boundary here, no other side, just a sea of darkness, with no horizon to trace, and a crumbling shore. He felt drawn to it, even though he knew the danger. He couldn't help but stare into it, as though a fundamental nothingness inside of him had recognized itself in the abyss. And at that moment, that something in motion began to move a little more boldly, separating itself from the dark.

And just before its first appendage stretched out of the inky abyss to wrap itself around Amos' ankle, he fled, backwards, knowing that he would become lost, but knowing that the alternative would be even worse…

#

He woke with a shock. It was morning in Vina's living room, and though she did not snore any longer, Amos recognized that she was still asleep by the shuffling of bedclothes and sheets. His head churned with wet static. He smelled like body odor and his breath had that sour taste that came with having eaten spicy food.

He quietly got to his feet, gathered up Tom's journal, and crept out the front door, closing it behind him.

A skittering of dead leaves along the sidewalk chittered to Amos as he entered their domain, like a group of children teasing him in a foreign language. The sun had yet to slink out of its hiding-place, and the world was still dyed in shadow.

He still had a few hours until the

landlord would be available to let him back into the apartment building, but if he was lucky again, perhaps someone would let him in.

By the time he got back to his stoop, clouds had screbbed in, and the sky had turned to a sort of gray paste. He reopened Tom Nero's journal and stared at the words, flipped through the pages. He pulled out his phone, made notes. Things that repeated. Lists.

Things like book titles, or names, or places, or songs. Amos felt that, maybe if he could get into Tom Nero's headspace, he could figure out where he'd gone, like how profilers could slide into the mind of a criminal. He had a list of clues, helpfully provided by Tom Nero himself, one of which was a piece of music.

Amos slipped his headphones in and navigated to Spotify, typing in *Ralph Vaughan Williams*. He scrolled until he found "Sinfonia Antarctica," which had been written in one of Tom's recent entries, and pressed play.

Almost instantly, the swell and sway of strings bloomed out of the silence between Amos' ears, and he leaned back against the steps to close his eyes. He was startled when a woman's voice, wordless and plaintive, struck out like a flashlight's beam across a blank landscape. Amos stared across the street at the park. It was a small green space, with a rusty carousel and playground for the kids. With the backdrop of the clanging bells and the dire music, it felt like something terrible was about to happen. Amos felt it rising in the back of his throat at the same time the woman's wordless vocals started up again. It was impossible to tell the difference between her and a shrieking Antarctic wind. He shuddered and plucked the headphones from his ears, instantly returning his world to a sort of gray, plain reality. The imagined scene, one of ghosts and creeping dread that he'd overlaid on top of the empty park, was gone.

He looked through the pages of the journal again. Here, there was a slice of paper ripped out. Amos wondered what could have been written there: perhaps a phone number, or an email? Some way to contact him? Amos realized he didn't

even know what Tom Nero's email was, if
he even had one, and then realized he
actually knew very little about the man
he'd been seeing, and he felt his heart
jump guiltily, like a fist curling around
red ropes of blood.

What if he'd been sent?

But that was impossible.

Amos chewed on a hangnail as his
eyes flew over the crabbed handwriting.
"Where'd you go, Tom Nero?" He asked no
one, and no one answered. "People don't
just disappear," he said, and a pigeon
bobbed by on the sidewalk. He watched
it, and it watched him back, its eye
unblinking. He felt penned in by the bird,
and his heart started to drum erratically
as it stopped directly in front of him,
staring at him with its head tilted to
one side, like a dog asking a question.

"Screb off," he said, distantly, to
the bird, and it obliged, taking wing
in a mottle of iridescent feathers. The
word was unfamiliar in his mouth, though
familiar in his brain, and he felt that
strange duality again. Amos swallowed
hard and attempted to move beyond the
weird feeling.

You should really be more careful who you give the keys to your life to, his internal voice chided him. *Who knows what Tom Nero might've found out about you? Maybe he's not disappeared from the world. Maybe he's just disappeared from you, ever think of that?*

It was possible, Amos had to admit. After all, hadn't he left everyone he'd known, and the life he'd had, all for what? This? A minimum-wage job, an identity that was less than rock-solid, and his writing. His hobby.

He thought he might be closer to getting into Tom Nero's head than he thought as he dug out a pen and opened to a fresh page of the journal.

Maybe if he could conjure Tom Nero on the page, he could conjure Tom Nero in real life. Just, *poof,* there he'd be, right in front of him, with that slippery screb on his face and that roguish, affected pose, one hand on his hip and one hand toying at his goatee. Amos dated the page and began to write.

screb.

He lifted the pen and looked at the word he'd written there. It was an utterly unfamiliar, yet somehow distasteful-sounding word. It could've been in a foreign language. It could've been the key to a code. It could've even been some kind of expletive. Amos found himself tracing the word, again and again, with the nib of the pen, until it was nearly graven into the page.

"Screb," he said, wondering at its sound, and instantly had the urge to scrub his tongue, his teeth, to purge his mouth of the foulness that had invaded upon saying the word. "Screb," he said again, and felt a distinct *loosening* in his gums. Faintly terrified, Amos maneuvered his tongue to the offending tooth and prodded at it. To his horror, the tooth wiggled in its socket, back and forth, and he sucked in a cold gasp of air that scraped his tongue clean. "Screb," he said again, distinctly. It sounded like a scrape of silverware across ceramic coming out of his mouth.

He set the pen back down and curled around the journal, writing with a sudden frenzy that astonished him.

screb screb screb screb screb screb

No matter what words came to his

mind, the only thing his pen would write was that single five-letter word, over and over again, until his handwriting didn't even look like his own anymore.

Someone coughed, and Amos looked up. Markos, the landlord, was standing there with a ring of keys in his hand. "You are needing key?"

Amos felt relief flood into him, and he opened his mouth, but then shut it, instantly, afraid of what word might come out. He nodded, and smiled in relief, and the landlord gave him a screb look. "I make spare for you. Here." Markos handed him a copy, and again, Amos nodded, trying to make his face a contortion of gratitude. "If you find other key, you will give back to me, yes?" Amos nodded again, more enthusiastically, and the landlord grunted and said something in Polish. "Very good day," Markos finished off, and then gestured to the front door.

Amos let himself in using the new key, and mounted the stairs as fast as he could, arriving at the third-floor apartment within moments. He opened the door and stepped inside, leaning against it as it closed behind him.

He exhaled, and then turned the lock on the door, taking some comfort in the simple motion.

People don't just disappear because you stop knowing them, Vina's chardonnay-soaked voice sloshed in his ear. *It's not a solipsistic world.*

But Amos knew better than that.

The hush and hot breath of his apartment washed over him. He opened his eyes and looked to the right. The photograph of the faceless man in front of the barn still hung where it was supposed to. Amos checked behind it. The box and the gun were both still present. Slowly, Amos sat down on the couch.

"Screb," he tried, and swore under his breath, looking at his trembling hands. That panic he'd felt while listening to *Sinfonia Antarctica* rose again, battering at his internal hatches. "Screb," he tried again.

He got up and moved to the laptop at his desk and sat down to type. The blank page of the word processor, a white monolith, stared at him challengingly. He put his fingers on the keys.

Screb screb screb screb screb screb

screb

He tried to force himself to type 'the quick red fox jumps over the lazy brown screb' but he couldn't. He could only write the word screb. He could only say the word screb.

He stood up, knocking the chair over, staring at the screen. Vertigo interceded, and he grabbed at the desk in a sudden rush of blood to the head. It was the same out-of-body sensation he'd felt upon coming across his own name in Tom Nero's journal. Amos-the-subject versus Amos-the-reader. An unfolding sensation, as if he was being vivisected, flayed open, all of his organs on display. He felt bare against the penetrating eye of the screb, whatever it was.

And it was then that he remembered his dream. The dark, dripping cave. The dark beyond the dark. The *screb* of the dark against the dark, moving purposefully towards him.

Amos screamed, and the sound came out as a whistling shriek, his mouth forced into the sibilant shape of an S against his will. *Screeeeeeeee!*

It was then that his phone began to

ring, and he snatched it out of his pocket, staring at the screen in disbelief.

TOM NERO was calling.

His trembling finger slowly landed on the green circle to accept the call, and slowly, his hand raised the phone to his ear.

Beyond, he heard nothing. Not even the whistle of the wind over empty plains. Not a single sound. He pulled the phone away from his ear, but the clock was ticking, counting off the seconds of nothing connected to his ear. "Tom?" He tried, almost snipping off the tip of his tongue with his teeth. He felt a huge unlocking inside of his chest, and his mouth was able to form a second word, and then they tumbled out of him as if they'd been dammed. "Tom, is that you? Where are you, Tom?"

Nothing answered. Not even the strange scratching screbs you hear on a dead phone line, the sound of electricity crackling and shifting over miles and miles. "Tom, it's Amos," he said, desperately. "Give me a sign. Tell me where you are!"

screb

Something moved, shifting in the blackness beyond his ear. Something intimate, but something foul, like a rapist's tongue.

Amos threw the phone away from him instinctively, and it landed on the couch, screen-up. He could still see the numbers ticking up on the clock. Could still hear the hideous, ancient thing as it screbbed and scratched its way up through the speaker.

scrrrrrreb

III.

Foreword to Vanishing Points: The Collected Work of Silas Monson

by Lem Shrowl

I didn't know Silas Monson. Most of the people who read his stories, his poetry, will never know Silas Monson, because he's disappeared from the world and left no trace behind, except for the very few people that knew him. His family, of course, Eugene and Ramona Monson, of Granger Lake, Georgia, are still living in perplexity as to their beloved son's whereabouts.

Most of you won't even know of Silas Monson. He's a relatively unpublished author, with a few short stories in anthologies starring far more notable writers. Monson, too, is notable, of course, for the fact that his absolute and total disappearance has become something of a literary mystery. Readers and lovers of unsolved mysteries have dug through his work, looking for the clues, the answers to his disappearance, thinking that there could perhaps be something someone missed, something hidden in the margins of the story. Monson is known for his wordplay, love of anagrams and crossing elements of one story with still others, blending to create a kind of fugue state while you read, entranced by the hallucinatory images that Monson conjures. One can almost feel the vines creeping through the house in "The Vines," an exploration of grief and interiority. In "Feed Me to the Foxes," a similar tale of grief and loss, Monson delves into an eerie relationship between a jailed convict's wife and the wilderness outside her door, as well as the wilderness inside of herself.

But it is only in the most recent story to come to my attention that really warranted the putting-together of this collection of work: "The Disappearance of Tom Nero." It was hotly debated whether or not this story would be included in this collection, but, dear aforementioned readers and lovers of mystery, your humble editor won the day and it is included in this collection. "The Disappearance of Tom Nero" was discovered in one of our slush piles by a particularly observant reader, and it crossed my desk only months prior to my writing this. It is, in my opinion, the definite answer to the disappearance of Silas Monson. In it, we are introduced to a character that has never before been seen in any other of Monson's work: the titular Tom Nero. It seems that Tom, too, has vanished.

It is unclear if the author is making a commentary on the fractious nature of authorship and entering into a post-metafictional universe by creating this story, though it does certainly seem as though Monson is tweaking our noses with it. I am certain that this fragment of a story will provoke a major response in the literary community, and I am curious to see how it will all screb out.

That will make screb after you read the story, of course.

As for Silas Monson, the investigation remains open. Did he simply uproot his life and vanish? Is he even now living somewhere peacefully, under a different sky? Was he even a real person, or perhaps just a pseudonym used by someone who is trolling the entire literary community? Or perhaps it is some ancient, elder thing from the darkness that is bent on erasing us all, one by one?

It is impossible to know. Perhaps this collection will provide a bit of immortality; for as long as the book is in print, Silas Monson hasn't disappeared – not entirely. His work still lives with us, and uncanny though it is, it never quite leaves your thoughts.

Whether that is a good thing, or a bad thing, is up to you, dear reader.

I hope you enjoy *Vanishing Points.*

ACKNOWLEDGMENTS

Tom Nero would not have disappeared if were not for the vigorous support of early readers—among the earliest, Demi-Louise Blackburn, Rosa Gir and Evelyn Freeling, who interacted with the manuscript from its very first incarnations. To read upwards of 10,000 words of someone's work unquestioningly is a rarity in workshop environments. I was lucky to find not one, but three such eager souls, and their belief in this piece was something I held to very tightly during storms of self-doubt.

For the artistry, my most heartfelt gratitude and appreciation goes to Alexis Macaluso for the brilliant interior illuminations, and to Leah Gharbaharan for the wonderful cover artwork. Both of them were a dream to work with throughout the process, and I could not be more thankful for their patience and genius.

Thanks must also be extended to Robert Ottone, publisher, who decided to take a chance with this manuscript—even after only reading a thousand words of it. Robert's curating an excellent series of work with Spooky House Press, as evidenced by his recent publications, and I am thrilled to be published alongside them.

Lastly: dear Mom, whose top shelf of Stephen King books drew me into the world of horror writing at a very early age. Hi, Mom. I love you.

ABOUT THE AUTHOR

TJ Price's corporeal being is currently located in Raleigh, NC, with his handsome partner of many years, but his ghosts live in northeastern Connecticut, southern Maine, and north Brooklyn. His work has appeared or is forthcoming in Nightmare Magazine, Pidgeonholes, The Bear Creek Gazette, The NoSleep Podcast, and various anthologies. He can be invoked at either tjpricewrites.com or via the blue bird @eerieyore. Failing that, one can make a circle of chalk on the floor, stand in the center, and burn a photograph of a loved one until all that remains is ashes. Then, listen for a murmuring from within the walls. Leave your message after the sound of the screb.

Also Available from Spooky House Press

Helicopter Parenting in the Age of Drone Warfare by Patrick Barb
The White Horse by Rebecca Harrison
Deeply Personal by Alexis Macaluso
Boarded Windows, Dead Leaves by Michael Jess Alexander
Her Infernal Name & Other Nightmares by Robert P. Ottone
The Disappearance of Tom Nero by TJ Price

Coming Soon

Her Teeth, Like Waves by Nikki R. Leigh
Residents of Honeysuckle Cottage by Elizabeth Davidson

CPSIA information can be obtained
at www.ICGtesting.com
Printed in the USA
BVHW061808180423
662584BV00017B/200

9 781959 946106